THE WHEEL

Tim Collins

Illustrated by Szabolcs Pal

BIG TOP OF HORRORS

ROY APPS

THE TANK
TIM COLLINS

THE WHEEL
TIM COLLINS

Badger Publishing Limited, Oldmedow Road,
Hardwick Industrial Estate, King's Lynn PE30 4JJ

Telephone: 01438 791037
www.badgerlearning.co.uk

The Wheel ISBN 978-1-78837-265-7

2 4 6 8 10 9 7 5 3 1

Publisher: Susan Ross
Senior Editor: Danny Pearson
Editorial Coordinator: Claire Morgan
Series Consultant: Dee Reid
Copyeditor: Claire Morgan
Designer: Fiona Grant
Cover Illustration: Mark Penman
Illustration: Szabolcs Pal

Tim Collins

Illustrated by Szabolcs Pal

Contents

Story Vocabulary
knife thrower
spinning wheel
audience

"Roll up! Roll up!" called the Ringmaster.

"Welcome to the Big Top of Horrors.
Enjoy the show, and if you're lucky,
you might even get to go home again!"

The audience laughed. They thought
the Ringmaster was joking.

But then strange things started to
happen…

Chapter 1

Stage Fright

Anna was watching the show in the Big Top.

It was very scary.

A knife thrower was throwing knives at the Ringmaster who was tied to a spinning wheel.

Swoosh.

A knife landed between the Ringmaster's knees.

Swoosh.

Another knife landed just below his left arm.

It's all part of the show, thought Anna.
No one will really get hurt.

Swoosh.

A knife landed right next to the
Ringmaster's face.

The knife thrower threw another knife.

This time it didn't land on the wheel
at all.

It landed right in the Ringmaster's chest.

Anna screamed.

Chapter 2

Join Us

The wheel stopped spinning.

The Ringmaster didn't move.

"Somebody help him!" shouted Anna.

But the audience just sat there.

Anna knew what she had to do.
She ran into the ring.

"Is he OK?" Anna asked the knife thrower.

The knife thrower laughed. "Of course,
not," she said. "He's dead."

Just then, the Ringmaster lifted his head and smiled.

Anna looked at him.

She could see right through him to the circles painted on the wheel.

The knife thrower pointed at the audience.

"They are all dead too," she said.

Anna turned to look at the audience. She could see through their bodies too.

They were all ghosts.

"Now it's time for you to join us," said the knife thrower.

She threw one of her long, sharp knives at Anna.

Chapter 3

No Way Out

The knife came straight at Anna.

She moved to the side and the knife only just missed her.

She ran for the exit.

"You must join us," shouted the knife thrower.

Anna got to the back of the tent.

This was where she had come in.
She was sure of it.

But there was no way out now. Just the thick, dark canvas of the tent.

The knife thrower was getting closer.

"There is no escape," she said. "You belong here."

Anna grabbed the edge of the tent. If she could lift it up, she might be able to get out.

But it wouldn't move.

The knife thrower was very close to her now.

Anna didn't know what to do.
She could feel her heart thumping.

Then she had an idea.

"OK," said Anna. "I give in."

She pointed to her heart, and said,
"throw it right here. Make it quick."

The knife thrower smiled.

She pulled back her hand and threw the knife at Anna.

Anna jumped to one side.

The knife stuck into the thick canvas.

Anna grabbed the knife and used it to rip a hole in the tent.

Anna jumped through the hole and landed on the grass outside.

She twisted her ankle as she fell, but she got up and limped away as fast as she could.

Anna felt sure the knife thrower would be behind her, ready to attack again.

But when she looked back, there was
nothing there.

The Big Top had gone.

There was just the sound of people
laughing.

Questions
Chapter 1

How does Anna feel as she watches the show? *(page 6)*

Where does the knife hit the Ringmaster? *(page 12)*

Chapter 2

Does the knife thrower care that she has hit the Ringmaster? *(page 15)*

Why does Anna get a shock when she looks at the audience? *(page 18)*

Chapter 3

What is Anna's idea? *(pages 24–27)*

What is surprising about the end of the story? *(page 29)*

About the Author

Tim Collins has written over 70 books for children and adults.

He lives near Oxford with his girlfriend, son and cat. His hobbies are listening to rock music and playing Pokémon GO.

He gets his best ideas on long walks.

About the Illustrator

Szabolcs Pal is a cartoonist who loves reading comic books.

He does not want to ever meet the Ringmaster!